All I Ever Wanted

A Novella

DAVID NETH

DN Publishing

All I Ever Wanted
Copyright © 2018 by David Neth
Batavia, NY

www.DavidNethBooks.com

Publisher: DN Publishing
Cover Design: DN Publishing
Editing: Steve Beaulieu
Proofreading: John Ognibene

ISBN: 978-1-945336-71-3
First edition

Subscribe to the author's newsletter for updates and exclusive content:
DavidNethBooks.com/Newsletter

Follow the author at:
www.facebook.com/DavidNethBooks
www.twitter.com/DavidNethBooks
www.instagram.com/dneth13

Also by David Neth

<u>Fuse series</u>
Origin

Omertà

Oblivion

<u>Small Town Christmas series</u>
A Christmas Reunion

<u>Under the Moon series</u>
The Full Moon

The Harvest Moon

The Blood Moon

The Crescent Moon

The Blue Moon

The Art of Magic

<u>Anthology</u>
Collateral Damage:
A Superhero Anthology

<u>Short Stories</u>
Limelight

Snow After Christmas

Chapter One

SOMETIMES I WISH I could have everything I've ever wanted. No worries about cost, practicality, or the realities of life. I wish life were more like a no-holds-barred, anything goes kind of living. Wouldn't it be perfect if we didn't have to worry about obtaining things we don't have? I think everyone would be happier if that stress was removed from their lives.

I keep this little fantasy of mine to myself, though. My mother would probably look at me with sad eyes and tell me to get a job if I wanted something. My best friend Genevieve—or Gen, as everyone who isn't her mother calls her—would nod and say, "Me too, Leo." Everyone else would think I'm stupid or just plain wouldn't care. Yeah, most likely that last option.

Which is why I don't voice this daydream to Gen when I spot a neat looking antique at the novelty store just out of town. Aptly called "The Barn" since the first store was in an old barn before it fell victim to a fire a couple years ago, the new store is much more modest, although it still has various knickknacks and antiques. We're on the hunt for the perfect Mother's Day gift, which is next weekend.

I used to make my mother all kinds of stuff to give to her as gifts. Without much money—or a father to help me out—it was all I could do. Maybe I'm getting lazier or just plain forgetful, but this year it snuck up on me and I have absolutely no idea what to do for her gift.

I have a small stash of cash leftover from working last summer, but it still needs to last another two months. After a day of wrestling with my options, I decided to use the money for my mom. She deserves something nice this year. She deserves it every year, but this year I can actually give her something special. I just wish I didn't have to pinch my pennies so much.

"Find anything?" Gen asks. Her brown hair is braided behind her back and she's wearing a black and green hoodie from her volleyball team.

I scrunch up my face. "I guess I could get her this vase thing."

The owner looks up from her book and says, "That's an outdoor planter. It'd be perfect in your mother's garden."

"Oh," I say. "That won't work." My face burns with embarrassment. I thought it was an umbrella holder.

We live in a small apartment above the drug store in town. The extent of our garden is a clumping of vines growing along the side of the building.

I eye up some of the handmade jewelry, but my mom doesn't wear much. I did see a set of earrings I thought Violet Dolan would like—the girl I've been crushing on since Christmas.

It's a long shot that I'd ever have a chance with her, being that she's one of the most popular girls in my grade and basically a social media icon. At least among our small town community.

"What about these?" Gen pulls my attention away from Violet. "Your mom could always use more potholders. They're handmade. And she loves purple, right?"

"Yeah, I guess." I take the potholders from her. "I was just hoping to get her more than this."

"So make her dinner too and you've got the perfect gift."

I sigh, still not satisfied. "Okay. I suppose that'll work. Did you find anything?"

"I'm thinking about getting these wind chimes. I figure she could put it out on the front porch so she can hear them when she's people watching."

I smile. Ms. Callaghan loves being on her porch. Even in the rain, she'll sit out and watch the water drip from the roof.

"There's some really cool stuff in here," I say as we meander back to the counter.

"Right? My mom loves it in here. I thought yours might too."

Everything in here seems to have a story. From the handmade pieces that clearly have a personal touch to the refurbished furniture, light fixtures, or decorations. Each piece is unique.

As we move to the checkout, something catches my eye. It looks like an old gravy boat. White porcelain with a golden rim and handle. This one even has an intricate blue floral pattern along the side. We had one that looked just like it, but my dad smashed it during one of their fights. It was my great-grandmother's.

"Hey, you coming?" Gen asks, noticing I'm not behind her.

"Hold on, I want to get this instead."

Gen flips over the price tag. "It's only ten bucks."

I beam. "This is perfect."

After cashing out, Gen and I hop on our bikes and make our way back to town. The weather is just starting to warm up and I plan to take advantage of it as much as I can. It's hard when you don't have your own backyard to enjoy the weather in.

I can't blame my mother, though. She never went to college. She started to, but then she met my dad, fell in love, and got married instead. Ten months later, I was born. That's why when Dad left two years ago, she didn't have any work experience other than the retail job she had up until I was born. So now she works weird hours at Target, which is about twenty minutes away.

If nothing else, it gives me peace and quiet to finish my homework most nights. Tonight, though, I decide to clean up the gravy boat and wrap it before Sunday. I can't wait to give it to her because I know it'll make her so happy. One of the hardest things for her—for us both, really—was parting with some of our family heirlooms for extra money. My dad ran off with most of our savings—both mine and my mom's—and since my mom has no siblings and her mother only has enough money left to pay her nursing home fees, we've been living paycheck-to-paycheck.

Pulling the gravy boat out of the newspaper the lady at the shop wrapped it in, I set it on the kitchen counter and adjust the temperature of the water so I can wash it off. It's dusty and glue remnants from the price tag are still there. Noticing the pile of dishes in the sink, I decide I probably better do them as well.

Half an hour later, the front of my shirt is wet, but the clean dishes are neatly stacked in the rack next to the sink. I grab the gravy boat and get to work. The lid seems stuck on and I can see dirt clogged in the corners of the spout. I pull out the wire brush from underneath the sink and work it into the spout, hoping the combination of warm water and soap will help loosen the top enough to really get in there and clean it.

As I work at the dirt with my hands wrapped around the outside of the gravy boat, I feel it start to tremble. I hold it still to make sure it's not going to slip out of my grasp and the trembling only gets worse. Smoke begins to seep out from the spout and I set it down, afraid it's going to burst.

I watch as the smoke continues to spill out, despite the water hitting it. I turn the knob to cold, hoping that'll help stifle any explosion.

Nope.

The dish continues to vibrate at the bottom of the sink as more and more smoke escapes, wafting up into the air. I wonder if the smoke alarms will sound, but when the scent reaches me, I don't smell anything burning. Instead, I smell sandalwood—and Palmolive, but that's on my hands.

Turning the water off, I take a step back as the smoke clusters above the sink. I watch in amazement as it forms into the shape of a person, becoming more and more defined and solid as the figure moves to the floor.

With my heart racing, I stare at the man standing in front of me. He's covered in soap suds that cling to his baggy red pants, which end just above his bare feet. His tan-colored shirt under his short black vest and gold chains around his neck is soaked and clings to his chest. Gold rings adorned his hands, some fingers even have two rings. Most notable of all, though, is the red ruby situated on the front of his turban.

After taking in his appearance and flicking away a cluster of bubbles, he snaps both his fingers and the suds are instantly gone. No bubbles, no sign that his shirt had ever been wet. My mouth hangs open at the sight of it.

He runs his dark hand over his short-cropped beard and smiles at me. All of his features seem to be darkened. Enhanced, almost. Like he's wearing make-up. It's even more pronounced when he smiles, which is probably triggered by my open-mouthed stare.

"Why, hello there. I'm Felix." He gives a low bow and adds, "Your wish, is my command."

Chapter Two

"HOW DID YOU...What are—huh?" I stammer ever so gracefully as I stare. This has to be a dream. How do I wake up? There's no way a man in a turban just appeared *out of a freaking gravy boat.*

He clutches his stomach as he laughs. "I should add that I'm Felix, *the genie.* The rings, the smoke, the mystique," he wiggles his fingers as his hands wave over himself, "it's all part of the package."

My eyes narrow. "Genie?" Yup, definitely a dream. What did I eat before bed? Actually, *when* did I go to bed?

He nods, a wide smile still spread across his face. "Uh-huh. In the flesh."

With a deep breath, I decide to humor him. "Okay fine. You're a genie. But where did you come from?"

Felix's brow scrunches and he looks around before his eyes land on the gravy boat in the sink. "Ah, there it is! You must've rubbed my lamp." Gingerly, he lifts it from the bottom of the sink and looks at it. "And that would explain the suds…"

I cross my arms. "What's going on?"

Tilting his head to the side, he asks, "Didn't you see me come out of the lamp?"

"I guess so, but that's not possible…" My voice trails off. Other than the man who just appeared out of thin air wearing a turban, this doesn't feel like a dream. But I saw him. But that still doesn't mean I believe it.

"All right, it sounds like you need a little help connecting the dots here." His ringed fingers rub his bearded chin as he thinks. His other hand sits just above the waist of his red pants. Finally, he wiggles his fingers in front of him before pressing them against his chest. "Okay, I'm a *genie*. You rub my lamp, I appear, offer you three wishes, once those three are up, I go back in my lamp until the next person rubs the lamp. You following me so far?"

I scowl at him. "I know what happens with genies, but… they're *fictional*."

He looks around dramatically before his eyes settle back on me. "Obviously not."

My phone buzzes on the counter and I cast Felix a warning look before I move to answer it. It's my mom. She calls every day on her lunch break. I can tell that she feels guilty for working such weird hours—and holidays—but it's what she has to do. I know that.

"Hello?"

"Hey sweetie, just calling to check up on you."

"Oooh, who's that?" Felix coos beside me.

I try to swat him away and act as casually as I can. "I'm fine. I just finished up the dishes."

"Who's there?" she asks.

"No one, it's the TV."

"Oh okay. There's some chicken in the fridge you can heat up for dinner."

"Okay." I keep a careful eye on the strange man raiding my kitchen. He's going through our cupboard and pulling out boxes of sugary cereals. Do genies eat? Maybe he's hungry.

"Did you get a lot of homework today?"

Felix finds the pack of Oreos and dives in.

"Uh, yeah, lots of homework. I should get started on that. Enjoy the rest of your break. Love you!" I hang up quickly to snatch the cookies away from Felix.

"Wha—?" He struggles to chew the three cookies shoved into his mouth.

"Get out of there!"

"Wowee," he mutters around the stack in his mouth.

After I close the cupboard door with the Oreos safely inside, I turn and study Felix. I want him to go away—especially before my mom gets home—but what he said intrigues me. What if this isn't a dream and he *could* give me what I wanted? I wait for him to swallow before pushing for more details.

"How do I know you're not lying?"

"Why would I lie?"

Good point. He didn't offer any stipulations in order to fulfill these so-called "wishes." Then again, how can I be sure this isn't just a dream? I try not to get my hopes up about anything.

"I don't know…"

He flashes a smile, his teeth black from the Oreos. "Watch." He motions to my T-shirt, wet from doing the dishes, and snaps his fingers. In an instant, it is completely dry.

I saw it, just like I saw him come out of the gravy boat, but I still don't believe it. I run my hand along the fabric of my shirt and feel for a trace of moisture.

"How did you…?"

He waves his ringed fingers toward him. "Genie."

"I don't need anything." It seems like the right thing to say. Especially when something sounds too good to be true.

"Everybody needs something." Felix motions around the room. "If this is the extent of your house, I could think of a few things you need."

Chewing on the inside of my lip, I consider the best retort.

"Listen, we might not have much, but we have what we need. So instead of insulting me and my family—"

"Whoa, whoa, whoa!" Felix puts up his hands as if to stop me. "I didn't mean to insult your family, buddy. Just trying to offer a few suggestions, that's all." He smiles again, which is getting annoying. Luckily, all traces of Oreo seem to be gone.

I was really hoping to give that gravy boat—or lamp, apparently—as a Mother's Day gift. Guess I'm back to square one with ten precious dollars wasted.

Suddenly, an idea strikes me and my stare softens. "Hey, could I transfer my wishes to someone?"

He shakes his head. "They're non-transferable, unfortunately."

"Oh." I consider this for a moment. "What about after I use my wishes? Could you leave the lamp for something else?"

Felix's eyes grow wide. "My *home*?"

"Guess not then." What the heck kind of genie is this?

When I don't say anything more, he says, "We're getting off on the wrong foot. I'm Felix, the genie. And you are?"

"No longer interested."

"Hey now, that's not nice. Was it something I said? I've been told I can be annoying, but I don't quite see it."

"Listen, if you disappear right now, I'll let you out tomorrow. Deal?" I need time to think about this. For whatever reason, I'm not waking up from this dream and I have the sneaky feeling that this *isn't* a dream, which means I need to somehow explain him to my mother without her putting me in the psych ward at the hospital.

He eyes me cautiously. "Promise?"

"Promise. Now get."

With slumped shoulders, Felix turns toward the sink but quickly turns back around. "What time are we talking tomorrow? Because I've been cramped in here for a while and I kinda like stretching my legs, you know? I'm getting older. My back is a nightmare. It's not as easy as it was—"

"I have school tomorrow. It won't be until the afternoon."

"Can't you let me out any earlier?"

"No, I have school. And then my mom will be home when I am."

"Your mother? How sweet! Is that who called you? I'd love to meet her!"

I huff. "You won't get to. I'll let you out as soon as I can tomorrow, but for now can you please get back in the lamp? I have homework to do."

Slumping his shoulders once again, he says, "Fine. But you should think of your first wish while you have me locked up like a caged animal."

I roll my eyes. "I'll think about it."

"And no more soap!"

"Okay!"

With yet another smile, he snaps his ringed fingers and immediately becomes a cloud of smoke that funnels into the spout of his lamp. Again, I smell sandalwood like the last time.

Wrapping the lamp in a dish towel—careful not to rub it—I carry it to my room and set it on my cluttered desk. Out my bedroom window, I make eye contact with my neighbor, Bruce. He's bent over laying mulch in the small strip along the side of his garage that used to serve as a flower bed. Since my other neighbor is a gas station, I often find myself looking out into Bruce's yard.

When he stands, I see his blue T-shirt is soaked through with sweat. He's a big guy so he typically sweats after any form of physical labor. He looks up and spots me so I give him a polite wave and quickly back away from the window.

Bruce is Gen's dad, but since her parents split up she doesn't like to talk to him much. His court-ordered visitation is about the only time she sees him. Apparently she never really liked him even when her parents were married. It's funny how even though she's my best friend, there's still a lot about her I don't know.

Chapter Three

THE OLD CAR horn ringtone on my phone blares loudly on the table beside my bed. I reach over quickly to shut it off and then stretch in whatever angle feels good, reminding myself over and over: *You have to get up. You have to get up. You have to get up.*

When I finally do open my eyes, I let out a yelp and scramble closer to my headboard.

Felix is kneeling beside my bed with his head resting on his folded arms. His face is inches away from mine—well, it was before I jumped back.

"Morning!" he shouts.

"Shh!" I press my finger to my lips. Lowering my voice, I ask, "How the hell did you get out?"

"Genie, kid." He smiles and sits up. "When you rubbed the lamp but didn't use all three of your wishes, you basically unlocked me. After the third wish is cast, I'm stuck in my lamp until the next person frees me. Which is why I can't just leave whenever I want."

My mind is still too foggy to process what he's saying but I hear my mother on the other side of the door.

"Leo? Are you all right, honey?"

Fearful she'll come in and see Felix—never mind the fact that I haven't dressed yet—I shout back, "Fine, Mom! Just stubbed my toe!"

"Okay, well hurry up. I'd like to see you before I go to work."

"I'll be out in a minute!"

When I hear the kitchen sink running, I turn back to Felix. "You told me you'd stay put until I let you out."

He shrugs. "I got bored. You don't know what it's like to be locked away for so long. You gave me a taste of freedom and it was delicious. Much like those cookies last night. Have any more?"

I sigh. I can sort of relate, but at least I have *some* freedom. "Okay fine, you can hang out in my room today—but don't leave the apartment. If my mom's home, you stay out of sight, got it?"

He nods. "Yes, master."

I frown. "Just call me Leo."

"Yes, sir."

I guess that's a little better. "You can eat if you're hungry, but don't go overboard."

I pull up my phone and check the time. It's getting late. I've usually had breakfast by now. Reaching for the blankets on top of me, I look up at Felix, who is still staring at me. "Can you go back in your lamp for a minute so I can get dressed?"

"Oh, I've been watching you all night. Sleeping humans are weird—fascinating—but weird. And I know I've been locked away for a bit, but isn't it a little late for the Christmas boxers?"

My cheeks flush and I try to hide my embarrassment with anger. "Just get in the lamp!"

His shoulders slump. "Okay, but you better be making a wish today!"

All I Ever Wanted

As the smell of sandalwood fills the room and I watch his body slowly fade to smoke and travel to the mouth of his lamp, I consider the prospect of the wish. Could he really grant whatever I wish for? Still seems too good to be true.

Dressing quickly, I close my door most of the way on my way to the kitchen. Felix said he'd stay in the lamp and out of sight, but after last night I can't be too careful.

"Who were you talking to?" Mom asks as she finishes up the dishes from breakfast. She's already wearing her red polo and khaki pants.

"Oh, um, Gen. She asked if I was walking to school today."

She nods and rinses a coffee mug that says, "Are you kitten me right meow?" I got it for her last Christmas because she was upset our landlord wouldn't let us have a cat. It got her to laugh, so mission accomplished.

Before I dive into my cereal I ask her, "What are your hours this week?"

"Mid-shift today, so if you can wait, I'll make dinner when I get home. Open tomorrow, off Wednesday, and close Thursday through Saturday."

"Six days?"

She chews on the inside of her cheek. "Yeah, I'm covering for someone else today. Can't turn down the hours. Plus, I figure you'll be in school, right?"

"Right," I mutter. My mom's always working. Or rather, she's always working crappy hours. Evenings, mostly. Working 2:30-10:30, so besides the mornings before school or the hour after she gets home from work at night, I barely get to see her. It's how she pays the bills, though, so I can't complain.

"HOW DID THE gravy boat turn out?" Gen asks as we fall in line with the other kids on the sidewalk heading toward the high school.

"Oh, it wouldn't come clean. Found a lot more than I bargained for inside." I can tell the truth a little bit.

"Gross. What are you going to do? You're running out of time."

"I know!" I grumble. "I don't know. Maybe I can come up with something. It sucks being poor, you know?"

"Yeah," she says.

We get to the corner and wait for the crossing guard to give us the go-ahead. Several of the kids in our group hold hands. Actually, Gen and I are the only pair *not* holding hands. Suddenly it seems like everyone at school is getting together. Except me.

My eyes drift up to the streetlight, anticipating its change, when I see the green light shift from a bright green to a dark teal…almost blue. My eyes bulge as I see a face appear.

"Three wishes!" he shouts down to me, which makes everyone look up.

"Did you see that!" Gen grabs my arm. "The light must be on the fritz, it looked like it was blue!" She laughs.

I force a smile, trying to hide my growing unease. "Yeah, pretty cool."

The rest of the day pretty much follows suit. Felix appears as a sketch on my English paper, he squeezes inside my gym bag in the locker room, and he even manages to make it into the frog we're dissecting in biology.

When I open my locker after biology, tiny hands grand my T-shirt and pull my head inside.

"Hey," I grumble.

"I just wanted to whisper sweet nothings in your ear," Felix says. "Seems like everyone around here's doing that."

I pull away and glance over at the couple next to me. They're staring at each other like they're going to be apart longer than just one period.

"Hey, where's your girlfriend?" Felix asks from my locker.

I lose it and stuff his shrunken body deeper into my backpack and zip it closed.

After slamming my locker shut, I turn on my heel and almost crash right into Violet. *Of course.*

"Sorry," I mutter.

She offers a tight smile and steps around me, throwing her blonde hair over her shoulder to readjust her bag.

I watch for a second before storming off to the bathroom. I hide out in the stall until the bell rings. Partly to be alone and partly because I'm still recovering from nearly plowing down Violet.

Once I'm sure it's quiet and there's no one in the room, I open my bag and let Felix out.

"Hey, hey, watch the merchandise," he says as he regains full size and straightens his turban.

"I told you to stay in my room. What are you doing following me around school?"

He looks away and his hands fidget. "I missed you." He even swings his leg slightly for effect.

"I didn't even know you existed twenty-four hours ago!" I whisper-shout.

"Well after watching you sleep all night, this might be a one-sided relationship, but I'm willing to work through that if you—"

"Stop! You want me to make three wishes, right?"

He nods. "Those are the basic fundamentals of a genie, yes."

"And that's the only way to get rid of you?"

"Get rid of me?" He repeats dramatically as a thin pink cloak emblazoned with rhinestones covers him. Swinging it over his shoulder protectively, he mutters, "I'm worth more than that!"

Pinching the bridge of my nose, I finally give in. "I'll make a wish, okay?"

Just one wish to test the waters. See if he's telling the truth. See what happens once I let him do his thing. I'm bracing myself for some sort of fallout, though.

The cloak vanishes and he beams. "You will?"

"Yes, but just give me a minute to word it properly." I've seen enough movies to know to watch out for loopholes.

He cracks his knuckles as he waits for me.

"Okay, I wi—No, wait. I can do it better." I chew on my thumbnail and think a bit more. "Leo Larkin requests—No, that's no good, either. Um…"

"Are you sure you're ready?"

"I'll get it!"

He crosses his arms and waits.

Sucking in a deep breath, I say, "I wish that I, Leo Larkin, had enough money that my mom and I didn't have to live paycheck-to-paycheck anymore."

"That's it?" he asks.

I nod. "That's it."

"Honestly, I thought you'd wish for an actual gravy boat for your mother or a new bike or a house or something. But money?" He shrugs. "Easy enough." Snapping his fingers, he smiles and says, "Your first wish has been granted, Master Leo."

I narrow my eyes, skeptical. Nothing happened.

"Are you sure?" I ask.

He shakes his head with a grin. "With a boring wish like that, you shouldn't expect more. If you wished for a pony, then you'd see some pizzazz." He spreads his fingers out and shakes his hands with an exaggerated smile. Jazz hands. This guy is a lot to take.

Still seeing the disbelief on my face, he says, "Call your mom."

"Why?"

"Just do it."

All I Ever Wanted

Watching him carefully, trying to hide the growing excitement that maybe he really *did* pull through on the wish, I pull out my phone and call my mom. She answers on the second ring.

"Leo? How weird, I was just going to call you. Anyway, you know how your dad borrowed some of your savings?"

Stole is more like it. Stand up guy, isn't he?

"Apparently he invested it all into the stock market and it took off. He just called and said he did that for you and that he's wiring you the money."

"Oh, cool." So I made an extra hundred dollars? That won't get me very far. Then again, I could use it to buy my mom a nice Mother's Day gift.

"Leo, I'm talking *a lot* of money. *A lot.*"

"And he wants to give it all to me?" That doesn't sound like my father. I'm used to him *stealing* money from me, not giving it to me.

"It's a little out of character, I know, but he said he always intended to give it back to you."

"Then why did he steal it?"

"I don't know, Leo, but he's giving it back—and then some! *A lot* more!"

The happiness and relief in her voice puts a smile on my face, but I'm still leery.

"Well, I'm not going to celebrate until the check clears."

She sighs. "I know he hurt us both badly, but he's still your father. And he's trying. You need to give him a chance. He could've kept this money for himself but he's giving it to you. Try to see the best things in people. Meet him halfway."

Chapter Four

TO MY SURPRISE, the money has already been deposited into my account like my dad promised. The number of zeroes astounds me and I'm reluctant to admit that it's Felix's doing, but what other explanation is there? Unless my dad really has changed, and that doesn't seem likely. I text him a 'thank you' anyway. He deserves that much.

"We should celebrate!" Mom grabs my hands and dances around the living room. I halfheartedly follow suit. "Let's go out to eat!"

It's been a while since I've seen her this happy, this relieved. Her joy radiates from her and it lifts my spirits too. I let myself indulge in the celebration.

"Even though it's a school night?" She's always been a stickler for being in bed at a decent time on school nights.

"Leo, this is really big news! We can't just ignore it! Where should we go? Anywhere you want!"

"Mom, we don't have to go out to eat. We can celebrate here." Ever since my dad left, we've had to watch every penny. Even now that I know my financial worries have been taken care of, I'm still reluctant to spend any money.

"Come on!" Her smile seems to be forever plastered on her face. "We have to do *something*!"

I smile at how happy she is. "Okay, okay. Let's just go to Applebee's or something."

"Are you sure?"

"Yeah, it's not too far and didn't you get that gift card for your birthday from grandma?"

"Honey, we don't have to use a gift card."

I press her cheeks between my palms. "Mom, that's what I want."

She tosses up her hands in surrender. "Okay, we can go there." She turns and fumbles through her purse. "I must've put the gift card in here somewhere."

Mom can't stop talking about the money the whole way there. About how relieved she is that my college fund is set, how I'm going to start off my adult life with my feet on the ground instead of swimming in debt, and how surprised she is that Dad willingly turned over the money—not before reassuring me that he loves me very much.

We're seated in the back, which is quiet, especially for a Tuesday night. By the time we order, she's begun to repeat herself.

"Leo, this will be a huge help for college! You can pretty much go wherever you want. You don't have to go to community college. Unless you want to, of course."

I smile. "Yeah, you won't even have to beg Dad for extra money."

She frowns and I immediately feel guilty for dampening the mood. "Your father had his own set of issues. I'm sure there are lots of reasons he left. You, especially, were not to blame."

I squeeze the balled up wrapper from my straw between my fingers and think about my relationship with my father. We don't really have one. Even when my parents were together, he never really showed much of an interest in me. He was just always there. And not 'there' in the way that a kid usually needs their father.

When he left, I didn't miss him. I didn't wish for him to come back. At least, not for myself. I just wanted my mom to be happy again. Tonight's one of the few nights that I recognize the old her.

"Do you miss him?" I ask suddenly.

She pulls her glass of water closer to her and sips through the straw. Likely stalling while she thinks of a good enough response. We rarely talk about my father, but I'm curious. Now that we're sort of indebted to him, I feel like he's open to discussion again.

"Yeah, actually. Despite everything, he was my best friend. We had problems, but everyone does. I guess I just miss having a partner."

I nod. "That makes sense."

She reaches across the table and grabs my hand. "But you and I are doing pretty well on our own, right? Sure, things are different. They're not ideal." She shrugs. "Your father leaving was just a bump in the road."

I'm quiet for a moment. She releases my hand and leans back, absently watching one of the TV screens.

"Do you think he'll ever come back?"

Her chest heaves as she breathes in a slow, deep breath. "I don't know. We'll just have to take it one day at a time. Whatever happens is not going to affect your future. I'm going to make sure of that." She looks at me until I meet her eyes. "You're all I need right now."

Trying to lighten the mood, I smile. "Well, enjoy it while you have it. I'm stuck with you. At least, for a couple more years before I ditch you for college. I *do* have that fat check, after all."

She laughs. "Gee, thanks!"

SURPRISINGLY, FELIX STAYED in his lamp last night…at least as far as I know. Maybe he kicked back and watched TV while Mom and I were at dinner, but there was no evidence of that when we got home. Even today, sitting in homeroom, there hasn't been any sign of him. Maybe using my first wish pacified him for the time being.

It's a shame too, because I think I know what I want for my second wish. After the success of the first one, I'm not as skeptical. I'm excited, even. There weren't any major repercussions from that money appearing in my account. I wonder if it was magic or if my dad really did invest the money in the stock market with the intention to give it back to me—but that seems like a pretty far stretch.

Gen echoes my doubts when I tell her about the money at lunch.

"Seems too good to be true." She pops open her chocolate milk and sips it before continuing. "Your dad left you high and dry a couple years ago without a word since and now all of a sudden you have all this money from him?"

I decide not to tell Gen about Felix because she'd probably just roll her eyes and call me crazy for thinking that I've *actually* met a genie. Talk about something being too good to be true.

"I don't know, Gen, but the money is in my account and I can't argue with that."

"He probably stole it. Drug money or something. My dad would probably do that." Ever since her parents split up, Bruce has been strapped for cash, chasing after one scheme or another since to get money fast.

"My dad's not a drug dealer." At least, he wasn't when he left. I scrape the walls of my yogurt container before asking, "What's the deal with your dad, anyway? I know you're not really a fan of his but I don't know if you ever told me why."

"He's just not a nice person. Never has been. He lies, steals, whatever it takes to better himself. As long as he looks good, he's happy. My mom and I are better without him."

"Yeah, but he's your dad."

"How often do you see your dad?"

"I, well—my dad *chose* to leave."

It's quiet while we both mentally retreat from the sensitive subject.

"What does your mom think? About the money?" Gen rolls up her taco and takes a bite.

"She's through the roof." I pull out my peanut butter and jelly from its bag. "Already has it earmarked for college."

Gen cocks her head. "Not a bad idea."

"I know. I just hoped she'd take some of it so she didn't have to work such stupid hours."

"I feel like your mom is one of those people who's going to work regardless of how much money she has. But I see what you're saying. It'd be nice if she didn't *have* to."

"Yeah." If my dad was around there'd be a second income. She wouldn't have to work as much. And she'd even have her best friend back. She's done so much for me, I can put aside my feelings for my father for a couple years if it'll make Mom happy. And the fact that he gave us so much money is a good sign that he's changed. If he really has, maybe my feelings toward him will too.

All I Ever Wanted

WHEN THE FINAL bell rings, I transfer books from my locker into my backpack, trying to divert my attention away from my locker-neighbor and his girlfriend kissing goodbye like he's going to war.

I stop as I grab my math book. It feels squishy and when I look, I see I'm grabbing a miniature-sized Felix around the legs.

"Ah!" I shout and let go of him.

He falls off the shelf in my locker and lands in my bag.

"What are you doing in there?" I mutter, trying my best not to draw attention to the fact that I'm talking to my locker. People are already looking in my direction from the shout.

"I listened! As long as I could! I stayed in the lamp, out of sight. But I got bored again." He stretches out, leaning against my gym shorts and putting his feet up on my history book. His shrunken body just barely fits the width of my bag.

He has a point. He's stayed out of the way for a while. And the first wish wasn't a total disaster.

"Thanks," I whisper. "And thanks for that wish. It worked."

"I know. It wasn't my first wish." He gives me a wink. "Ready for the second one?"

"Who are you talking to?" Gen appears at my right with her backpack slung over one shoulder.

"Oh, no one." I hastily zip my bag shut and hear muffled complaints from inside, so I say quickly, "Wanna walk home together?"

She giggles. "We usually do."

Pulling on my bag, I follow her down the hall. When we pass Violet and her friends at her locker, she smiles at me, but I quickly look away.

"What are you doing tonight?" Gen asks once we're on the sidewalk and get stuck behind another couple joined at the hip.

"I don't know. I have some homework, but it's Mom's night off so she'll probably want to do something."

"That's cool. Have you talked to your dad at all since he gave you the money?"

I shake my head. "Not really. I texted him 'thank you,' but he didn't reply. He must've been busy. He called my mom when he first told us about the money."

"Maybe you should call him."

"I might." Mom will probably insist. I'm surprised she didn't yesterday.

"I think it's sweet that you're so worried about your mom's happiness."

I smirk. "Thanks."

"I know things aren't the way you want them right now, but things will change. Your mom will find someone else."

"Yeah, I know. It's just…sometimes I wish my parents were back together, you know? Then we wouldn't have to worry about money and Mom could be happy again."

We come up to the crosswalk and fall into silence as we stand in the crowd. Once we're heading down Main Street toward my apartment, Gen replies as if there wasn't a break.

"The grass is always greener, Leo. Don't wish away something you have for something that might be."

Wish. I said, *wish*. I stop in my tracks as my eyes grow wide. Oh no. Oh no no no no no.

She looks back at me. "What's the matter?"

"Uh, nothing. I think I forgot some of my homework at school."

"Oh, you can copy mine tomorrow. It's fine."

I keep my eyes on the sidewalk and nod as I resume walking. My mind worries whether Felix was still in my bag when he heard us talking. My heart races and I try to calm myself by saying he left when I closed the bag. Try to replay my conversation with Gen. Try to convince myself I didn't say what I think I said.

We're quiet the rest of the way back to my apartment, which isn't far.

"Call me before you leave tomorrow so I can give you my homework before class."

I nod. "Yeah, okay. See you tomorrow."

As I walk up the steps above the drug store, I don't notice anything out of the ordinary, but I still feel like something's off. The world seems quieter, slower. It might just be in my head, but I swear the trip up the staircase is longer than it usually is.

When I walk through the door to the living room, it's empty, but I can hear voices from the kitchen.

My mother's and a man.

I know that voice.

I close the door and step into the kitchen. The man is wearing a dark gray long-sleeved shirt and jeans. He looks back at me and I see his stubbly face as he smiles.

"Son. It's been a while."

Chapter Five

MOM COMES AROUND from behind the counter and approaches me. There's a look of hesitation on her face, but it's the hand that lingers on my dad's shoulder that catches my attention.

"Honey, we need to talk," she starts.

It's clear that I'm wearing my surprise on my face, so I look down before forcing a smile. "It's fine. We'll talk later. You're busy."

In a move that would impress the power-walkers at the mall, I escape to my room, narrowly dodging my mother's reach.

Once the door is closed, I lean my head against it and let out a deep breath as I stare at the ceiling.

Why? Why would I be so reckless to say 'wish' when I had *just* been talking to a genie? I'm so stupid. I potentially just messed up my mom's life because of one mistake. I sink to the floor and stare at the carpet between my legs. The weight of the guilt is almost tangible.

All I Ever Wanted

To be honest, I'd been considering this for my second wish, but I wish—no, I *should've* been more careful, paid more attention to getting the wording right so things would be different. Better. Now I'm stuck with the literal interpretation of a passing comment.

I'll need to be more careful with the third wish—*if* I even decide to make a third wish. I wonder what'll happen if I break Felix's lamp. Just set it on fire or let a bus roll over it or something. Would that kill the source of his power or would I just remove the very thing that guarantees I'll never have to see him again after this is over?

Hopefully he doesn't leave too much of a wreckage in his wake.

"Why so glum, chum?" Felix asks in my ear.

I jump and scramble to my feet.

"Honey, are you okay?" Mom calls from the kitchen.

"I'm fine!" I turn toward Felix, grabbing him by the stupid gold chains around his neck and pull him closer. I drop my voice and mutter, "You told me there weren't going to be any tricks!"

"Whoa, easy," he replies in a forced high-pitched voice. "You said the magic words. You knew the rules. It's not like I pulled this wish out of nowhere!"

"You have no idea what you've done."

Mom was devastated when Dad left the first time. She was just getting back to her normal self and now this.

Sucking in a deep breath, I let go of his chains and mutter, "Sorry."

He brushes off imaginary dust from his shoulders. "Your mom was just saying how she misses your dad. Isn't he also the reason you made your first wish?"

Annoyance bubbles in me, though I'm not too surprised. "Where did you hear that? Have you been following me?"

Felix holds up his hands in a surrender gesture. "I just

wanted to be available if you wanted to make a wish."

"So you've been *waiting* for me to slip up like this?" I take a step toward him.

"Well, I—" He steps back against my dresser and the tin can that holds my change rattles.

"You never thought of *verifying* the wish before you granted it?"

"It's not in my nature."

"Do you have no self-control that you'll just grant wishes whenever you feel like it?"

"Well, there are rules—"

"Leo, what's going on in there?" Mom asks again. "I'm coming in."

I look at the door in a panic but when I turn back to Felix, he's gone, only the smell of sandalwood remains.

"Honey, who are you talking to?" I'm facing my dresser and she watches me quizzically. "Were you burning a candle?"

"No," I spit, more venom lacing the word than I intend.

Tilting her head out the door, she says, "Come out here and let's talk."

"I don't want to talk."

She closes her eyes and sighs. "Your father's not here. He went to get us dinner."

I can't shut her out like this. Clearly, she senses I'm bothered by this, but not for the reasons she thinks. If she wants to get back together with Dad, then fine. But I want to be 100% sure that she *actually* wants to. Of her own free will. No genie influence at all. That's the way I would've worded the wish if I had realized Felix was still in my backpack.

The silence isn't helping any, though.

"How did this happen?" I ask.

She takes a seat at the end of my bed. "Well, we reconnected when he called about the money. We talked for a long time.

Found out he's been working in Pennsylvania. That he's been going to his meetings. That there was an opportunity for him to transfer up here and he was considering taking it. For you. For us."

"Then why did he leave in the first place?"

"Come here." She pats the spot beside her.

After I sit she puts her arm around me and leans her head against my shoulder.

"Sometimes, for some people, everything just seems to be building up in their lives. Like a pressure cooker. Your father had a lot going on at the time. He was under a lot of stress at work, not to mention his drinking, and, to him, it seemed like the world was against him. He just needed to escape. But he loves you and he missed us. So he's back."

"And you're okay with this? Him just showing up like this?"

"I offered to have him stay here."

I try to think of it from my mother's side. Is this really what she wants or is she just trying to bring my father back into my life? Trying to make it easier on us financially?

"Are you happy?"

She takes a deep breath. "Yeah, I am." Lifting her head, she looks me in the eyes. "The family's back together. It'll take some work but we'll get there."

That's for sure. I'm not as easy to forgive as my mother is. My father's scorned me too many times through the years to allow him back into my life so easily.

But I also trust my mother's judgment. If she says Dad is different, then I need to at least give him a chance to prove me wrong. Maybe he's not as much of an ass as I remember him being.

"I just don't want to see you get all mopey again," I confess.

She gives me a sad smile. "I know. I appreciate you looking out for me, but it's *my* job to take care of *you*. Take put more pressure on yourself than necessary."

I study my hands in my lap. "Yeah, I suppose you're right."

Mom and I talk for a bit more, hypothesizing what the future holds for us. Bringing Dad back into the fold, what we'll do with the extra money after college is paid for, whether she'll quit her job.

It isn't until I hear Dad announce that he's back that I realize my stomach is growling.

"Let's go eat," Mom murmurs and leaves the room.

Dinner is very quiet at first—my mother talking the most, trying her best to start a conversation.

"Jim, tell Leo about this new job."

"It's just another construction job. Pays a bit more, but it's the location that really sold me. Especially since your mother offered to have me stay here."

Not much new to go on, but I need to make the effort. "Is that what you've been doing?" One look at my mother and I see a big grin on her face.

Dad shrugs. "More or less, yeah. What about you? What have you been up to? Any girlfriends?"

I shake my head. "No, mostly just school."

"Leo is in the top of his class," Mom adds.

I roll my eyes. "Number fifteen out of a hundred. It's not that big of a deal."

"Must be working hard, though," Dad says.

"Actually, my summer job doesn't start for a couple weeks."

"Oh, you're working now?"

My cheeks flush as I realize I misunderstood him. "Yeah. Had to, really."

Mom clears her throat. "There's more pizza here. Help your-selves."

"Do you like what you do?" I try to change the subject away from our previous money troubles.

Dad shrugs. "It's a job. I guess I'm good at it, you know? Been doing it pretty much since I was your age."

"Really?"

"Yeah. My old man used to take me around wherever he went. Didn't take long for me to catch on."

Talking to him is actually easier than I thought it'd be. I used to think that if I ever saw him again, I'd give him a piece of my mind. Yell at him for leaving my mother a mess. Forcing her to work ridiculous hours in order to put food on the table. How we had to move out of our house into a tiny apartment because he never once sent any sort of alimony or child support check.

But now, sitting across the table from him, I'm discovering that I'm willing to try to learn more about him. What he's been up to; discover the man my mom sees in him. I've built him up to be such a villain in my head that I don't think I've been giving him a fair chance before this.

So that's what I'm going to do. This may have been an accidental wish, but it was my wish nonetheless. This is the way the cards were dealt, so I'm just going to have to play my hand.

Mom and Dad retreat to the couch after dinner, but I turn in. It's getting late and I still have some homework to do. Besides, I think I've had enough of the reunion for one night. It's almost like there's a stranger spending the night and I have to be on my best behavior.

I don't jump or react at all when I see Felix in my room. He's sitting at my desk, rifling through one of the drawers, but stops immediately when he sees me.

"Uh, you left it open and something caught my eye."

"It doesn't matter." I close the door and lay back on my bed. My mind is wrapped up in my parents. Their reunion, their life before their split, how they got together in the first place. They were young when they started dating. Teenagers. My age.

The longest relationship I've ever had was with Heidi Otis. It lasted two weeks at the end of my summer job in August. I had been flirting with her all summer and nothing happened until *she* asked *me* out. By the time school started again, we both went back to our normal friends and things fizzled.

Meanwhile, it seems like everyone else is pairing up. Especially as the school year winds down and other kids start making plans for the summer. It makes me wonder if I'll ever find someone or if I'll end up alone. Or worse, if I'll have to settle just so I'm not alone.

Does that make me shallow? Is it bad to hope to end up with someone beautiful, like Violet?

"Felix," I start in a small voice.

"Yes, sir."

"You can grant any kind of wish, right?"

"Well, there are some limitations. Immortality, world domination, enslavement, those are my no-no squares."

"What about love?" I keep my eyes on the ceiling, too embarrassed to look at him directly, even if I know I'll never see him again after my next wish.

He jumps on the bed beside me—closer than I'd like—with his head propped up by his arm and a giant smile on his face.

"Who's the lucky girl?"

"What?" I glance at him as the bed settles after his jump. I force myself to look back at the ceiling, trying to be indifferent. "There is no girl."

"Boy?"

"Shut up!" I get up and close my desk drawer.

"I'm only teasing, sir. Look, love is weird. Even without my influence. I can put two people together, but there's no promising that they'll hit it off."

"Oh." I try to hide my disappointment. "That makes sense. I was just wondering."

"*Is* there someone?"

"Yeah."

"And there's nothing else you want to wish for? Consider this my verification, by the way."

I smirk. "I wish I could go on a date with Violet Dolan—even if it's a short one. Just so I know whether or not I even have a chance with her."

Felix offers a sad smile. "It's your last wish."

I look down at my feet. "Yeah, it is."

"So…this is the end for us."

"Yeah." I don't want to tell him that I'll miss him. I won't. At least, I don't want to. I've known him for a few days. That's it. In that time he's been a thorn in my side, but he's forever changed my life.

"You're one of my favorites," he says.

I look up at him with a grin. "I am?"

He nods. "Uh-huh. Most of my masters are demanding or demeaning. You treat me like a real person." He sucks in a deep breath. "But, I'm just wasting your time now." Raising both his hands up, he says, "Your wish," he snaps his fingers, "is my command."

Almost instantly, my phone rings.

My head snaps to Felix and he says, "I'm just *that* good."

Nervously, I answer it.

"H-Hello?"

"Um, Leo? It's, uh, Violet. I'm in your English class."

"Right—yeah—I know."

"Are you busy? Do you want to hang out?"

"Right now?" My voice jumps an octave.

"Oh yeah, I guess it's kind of late. I just had to ask while I still had the courage." She giggles. "If you can't, I understand."

"No! I can meet you somewhere."

"Cool."

"Uh, where?" I ask.

"Oh, I don't know."

"How about, um, by the railroad tracks. We could watch the stars." Ugh, how cheesy.

"The railroad tracks?"

I replay what I said in my head and turn pink. It's worse because Felix is watching me with a big grin on his face. Asking a girl to meet me by the railroad tracks at night? Nope, that doesn't make me sound like a murderer at all.

"You mean at the end of Prospect?" she adds.

"Yeah, but I understand if you don't want to. I mean, I don't think it'd go over well if you came here and it'd probably be the same at your place." At least I manage to avoid saying, "My mom won't let me."

"Yeah, it's probably not a good idea," she says. "I can meet you there. Say, in like fifteen, twenty minutes?"

I nod and then add, "Sure, yeah. Sounds good. See you there. Bye!" I hang up the phone and drop it on the bed, my hands shaking.

"Look at you, stud! Getting a girl to sneak out of the house for you."

Crap. I didn't think about how *I'd* get out. The only exit is through the living room, where *both* my parents are. What a turn of events. The rare night my mom is home and I can't sneak by while she's passed out by the TV because my *dad* is here.

"How am I supposed to get out of here?"

Felix pats my shoulder. "Consider this part of the last wish, but it's just this once, okay? Take care of yourself, kid."

Before I have time to respond, he snaps his fingers and I instantly feel the cold chill from the outside air. I'm standing alongside the railroad tracks at the end of Prospect Street. Alone. No sign of Felix or Violet anywhere.

Within ten minutes I see Violet walking up the street with a white sweater wrapped around her slim body. Her long blonde hair is collected to one side of her head and her arms are crossed over her chest.

"Hey," she says with a smile when she sees me.

"Hey."

She lifts her shoulders. "So, what did you want to do?"

"I thought we could watch the stars, but I realize I didn't bring anything to sit in."

That's when I smell the faint scent of sandalwood and notice two folding chairs appear in a puff of blue smoke behind Violet. Felix must be stretching the "first date" wish out.

"But these look pretty decent." I step forward and pull them out.

"Thanks," she says when I offer her the first open chair and move on to the next. She takes a seat in hers and I open mine up to sit beside her.

We look up at the sky. It's cloudy at first, but suddenly they begin to part.

"Wow," she says. "It's beautiful."

"Yeah, it really is unbelievable, isn't it?" I say.

"Can't say I've ever really paid attention to the stars too much," she admits. "Usually when I'm outside this late it's for a bonfire. Can't wait for those this summer. Do you remember Joni's last year? That was crazy."

"Uh, no," I say. "I don't really know Joni, so I wasn't invited."

"Oh."

"So..." I say, ever so eloquently to try to continue the stalling conversation.

"So..."

"What made you call?"

She shrugs. "I don't know. I guess I've been thinking about you a lot lately."

I huff. "Because I almost ran into you? Sorry about that."

She chuckles. "It's okay. I always just assumed you were with Genevieve, but I wasn't sure. Anyway, tonight I was just thinking, screw it, if you're dating her, you'll tell me." She smiles. "But you're not."

"No, I'm not." I can't help but wonder how many people just assume that I'm dating Gen. That train of thought doesn't last long because here I'm with Violet Dolan. *The* Violet Dolan.

"And I'm happy about that," she continues.

I look over at her with a smile. "Oh yeah? Why's that?"

"Because I get to do this."

Violet leans in and kisses me. Her lips are barely on mine for a second before her chair cracks and her body topples onto mine. She sinks to the ground laughing.

"That went better in my head," she says.

I laugh and offer my hand to help her up. "Not the most graceful first kiss I've had." I wonder if Felix had anything to do with it.

She gets to her feet and holds onto my hand. "We could try for a second one."

With the laughter having broken the tension, I feel a surge of courage and lean down to kiss her. Much better this time. Longer, too.

We sit and watch the sky some more. Since Violet's chair is broken, she sits in my lap and steals a couple more kisses before we decide to go home.

"It's getting late," she says.

My grin is plastered on my face. "Okay."

We walk down the sidewalk hand-in-hand, talking about anything and everything. What she's doing for the summer, our teachers, cheerleading, how I can't find anything for my mom for Mother's Day, which is this weekend.

I'm too embarrassed to tell her I live above the drug store, so I follow her down toward her house. She stops me three houses down from hers.

"It's better if my dad doesn't see you." She plants a quick kiss on my cheek. "I'll see you at school tomorrow."

Chapter Six

READY TO GO? Gen texts me the next morning.

Sorry! I have an errand to run this morning, but I'll see you there!

I bid my parents a farewell and head downstairs. Right now, I don't even care that they're back together. I'm focused on Violet. I want to head down to the bakery and buy her something. A cookie or a muffin or something. Nothing too big, but something that'll serve as a 'thank you' for the good time last night. Besides, even if I wanted to go big, it's not like money's an issue.

Luckily, despite the shrinking number of businesses in our small town, we still have a bakery. It should really be named Phoenix Bakery because they announced they were closing, had a big sale and the uptick in customers kept them open.

I step in and look over the options behind the glass. I have no idea whether Violet prefers chocolate chip or peanut butter or maybe oatmeal raisin. But then, being a cheerleader, she probably isn't keen on having sweets so early in the day. Maybe a muffin is a better option. But should I get blueberry or chocolate chip?

Right, the sweets. Blueberry it is.

When I hand the cashier my card to pay, she swipes it and then frowns. "Hmm, says insufficient funds."

"What? That's impossible."

I don't have any other money on me, but the money my dad put in my account should be more than enough. Did he renege?

"Try again."

Another swipe and she shakes her head.

"Excuse me a minute." I step outside and call my mom.

"Hi sweetie," she says. "Are you at school already?"

"Not yet," I say. "I wanted to get a muffin on my way but my card's being denied." Best not to tell her about Violet. Not yet, at least.

"Oh, I'm sorry," my mother says on the other end.

"What happened to the money I got the other day?" It's also probably not a good idea to throw accusations toward my dad. I'm trying to accept him back in my life for Mom. I can't blame him for everything.

"Oh, I told you. That's for college."

"All of it?"

"Well yeah. I put it in a separate account so neither of us would be tempted to touch it."

"Mom!"

"Honey, you're going to be thankful when you don't have any student debt. Trust me. The muffin can wait."

"But—"

"Have a wonderful day at school, darling!" She hangs up and the matter is settled. All that money I got is out of my reach.

First. Wish. Wasted.

AT SCHOOL, I go straight to Violet's locker. She's tucking her hair behind her ears to show off a new set of earrings to her friends. Fancy dangling ones.

"Oh, those are *so cute*!" Nancy Doyle says. Leanna Gregory basically echoes her friend, but all conversation ceases when I approach.

My throat instantly goes dry and my palms are sweaty, but I force out, "Hey."

Violet smiles and looks down. "Hey." She runs her fingers through her long hair.

Nancy and Leanna giggle and she shoots them a look. Immediately, they turn and scurry off down the hall, clutching their books to the chests and giggling to each other.

I ignore them and turn back to Violet. "Last night was a lot of fun. We should hang out again soon. Maybe tonight?" Too bad I couldn't get that muffin for her this morning. Or flowers. Maybe then this wouldn't be so awkward. Of course, it would also draw more attention to us.

"Uh, yeah. Maybe." She looks down at our feet and I notice a few other kids looking in our direction.

"Is tonight not good for you? We could hold off until this weekend if that's better," I offer.

Out of the corner of her eye, she looks over at the group of kids a few lockers down and then looks in my direction, but still doesn't meet my eyes. "Look, I've, uh, been really busy lately, so I don't know if I'll have the time."

I nod and quickly add, "Oh, right, yeah. Of course. I've been busy with, um, stuff too."

"Yeah, so you understand that it's probably not a good idea if we..." She trails off.

"Oh." I force a smile to hide my disappointment. "Oh yeah, sure. No, that makes sense. I totally get it. It's no big deal, really. I'm fine."

She offers a sad smile. "Well, I'll see you around then."

"Sure thing." I spin on my heels and retreat to my locker, keeping my head low to avoid the looks from everyone who saw me get thoroughly shut down.

I should've known is wasn't ever going to work out with her. Violet's out of my league but last night I thought I had a chance.

The dynamic between us was different today. The connection's gone. Last night she seemed to have a genuine interest in me. Today, she seemed embarrassed to be seen with me. I really thought something would happen once I got her alone and talked to her. Especially since *she's* the one who called *me*. And she kissed me, even. Several times.

Granted, that was fueled by a wish granted by my genie, but it still sucks to watch my expectations crumble.

Is Felix still even *my* genie? I haven't seen him since he popped me out of the house last night. I better not see him. Not with two of my wishes failing. At least my mom's happy.

My first two classes seem to drag and my mind wanders, thinking about ways I can still make these wishes work for me.

I consider going to a community college like I'd planned so I can pay cash for it and still have money leftover, but I don't think my mom would be happy about that. She's always saying how she wants me to do better than her in life and even though I'd still be going to college, getting a two-year degree simply so I can have faster access to my savings would be the easy way out.

Something my father would do. That thought alone makes me shudder.

As for Violet, I could approach her again in a more discreet location. Maybe just call or text her. That way, she wouldn't have to be embarrassed while I'm schmoozing her. The question is, *how* would I schmooze her? And what happens if she never gets over her embarrassment of me? I don't want to be with someone who ignores me in front of her friends.

What's most frustrating of all is I haven't seen Gen yet today. I went right to Violet's locker when I got into school. Usually we hang out before classes start because lunch is the first period we have together. But she's in all of my afternoon classes, so I'll see her eventually.

When I finally get to the lunchroom, I spot her sitting at our table and take the seat next to her.

"I have so much to tell you." I dig into my brown paper bag and grab my sandwich. Gen seemed excited for me with the last girl I dated, so I'm anxious to tell her about Violet. Hopefully she'll have some advice for me.

"If it has anything to do with Violet, I don't want to hear it." She keeps her eyes on her lunch and doesn't look at me.

My face drops. "What's wrong? Where'd you hear about me and Violet?"

"So it's true, isn't it?" Finally, she turns to me and I can see how hurt she is. "You and Violet hooked up last night?"

My mouth hangs open as I stutter. "I—Gen, it's—no, we didn't *hook up*—who told you all this?"

Her voice grows. "It's all over school!"

My cheeks flush. "Oh." That must be why Violet was so embarrassed this morning.

"I just thought you'd have a little more respect for me and tell me yourself instead of having to hear it from *everyone* else." She starts to pack up her lunch, as if she's going to get up and leave.

"Gen, wait, what's the matter?" Some heads in the lunchroom start to turn toward us. Look-At-Me Day, apparently. But right now I don't care how many people stare. I care about what my friend is so upset about.

"Isn't it obvious?" She gets up and flings her hair over her shoulder. "I've been your best friend for *years* and then you ditch me for *her* and…" She takes a deep breath. "I just thought we were closer than that."

She turns and weaves around the tables and rushes out of the room.

I sit dumbfounded in her wake. How long has she felt this way? Should I have asked Felix for a first date with Gen? Would I have even needed to use a wish? Would I even *want* to go on a date with Gen?

That's a stupid question. She's my best friend. I always love hanging out with her.

But she's right. I *did* ditch her. Without a second thought, even. I've been a horrible friend to her and I can't help but think it's all Felix's fault. If I hadn't found that gravy boat, or whatever it is, I wouldn't have been so greedy. Life would've gone on, just as it always has, and I wouldn't have hurt my best friend.

GEN MUST'VE GONE home early because I didn't see her the rest of the day, which makes this walk home from school seem twice as long. I feel bad and I can't get what she said to me out of my head. Or how she felt when she heard. I've been trying to dig up memories, trying to pull out some clues that would indicate that she ever had feelings for me, but there's always an excuse for each instance. Maybe I've just been self-absorbed for a long time.

I consider going right to Gen's house, but my stomach is aching with hunger. Besides, I've been thinking up my apology. I'll show up to her place tonight and tell her how if I would've known she felt that way, I wouldn't have ever gone out with Violet…or something like that. It sounded grander in my head. I still have time to figure it out.

Even before I unlock the door at the bottom of the stairs, I can hear shouts coming from our apartment. It only grows louder as I climb the stairs. When I enter the living room, I see the remote control for the TV soar through the air and slam against the wall. The batteries fly out before it lands on the carpet.

Both my parents turn to me when I enter, my mother looking sorrowful, my father looking angry.

"Leo, I didn't think you'd be home this early," Mom says, putting her hands on her hips in an attempt to act casual.

"Same time every day."

"Why don't you go outside and play while your mother and I have an adult conversation?" Dad says with an edge. Like he's mad at me for interrupting them. I'm very well accustomed to this tone.

Mom shoots him a look. "Please, he's not an idiot. Don't talk to him like that."

"I'll talk to him however I want after the money I just gave him."

"Don't you *dare* hold that over his head!" Mom snaps. "You *stole* that money from him in the first place!"

I haven't seen her like this since Dad left the first time. Angry, protective, frazzled. I'll take a depressed mother over a stressed one any day.

"What's going on?" I ask, my voice small.

"Just go to your room!" my father barks.

"It's his house, he can go wherever he wants to go. Maybe *you* should be the one to leave!"

"That's not what you were saying the other day when you convinced me to come back." My father raises his voice into an unnatural falsetto. "'We miss you. Leo needs a father. I can't do it on my own.' And now that I've uprooted my life, you're trying to tell *me* to leave?"

"What about *our* lives? We had to sell the house, Jim. Our

son doesn't even have a back yard anymore!"

He cusses at her and she gives it back to him.

"Just get out of here," she tells him, pointing to the door. "Come back when you're ready to be a decent human being."

His jaw clenches as he stares at her. Then, without a word, he disappears to my mother's room, grabs his bag, and walks out the door with a slam.

There's a definite silence after he leaves. A noticeable shift in the room. The source of tension is gone so my mother wraps her arms around me.

"I'm sorry, honey," she mutters as she squeezes me. "I never should've asked him to come back."

"It's okay."

"No, it's not." She pulls away and takes my face between her hands. There are tears in her eyes. "We were doing okay, just the two of us. We were getting there."

"I thought you were happy? I thought this is what you wanted so you weren't so lonely?"

She frowns and wipes at her eyes. "I thought so too, honey."

"So why did you ask him to come back?"

"I guess I just liked the idea of having him back. Someone to fall asleep with on the couch, someone to sit with me when you walk across the stage at graduation, someone who would be just as proud of you as I am. But when it came down to it, your father just isn't that person. I guess he wasn't what I really wanted."

Chapter Seven

LAYING IN MY bed, I stare at the ceiling while I think about the week so far. I stumbled on a genie, was convinced to make my three wishes, and they all turned out to be crap.

My life isn't any better than it was. If anything it's worse now. I knew what to expect before. I knew the trajectory my life was going. Now? Now I have no idea.

I wish I never found that lamp. I wish I'd never met Felix. I wish my life could go back to the way it was a week ago.

If only those wishes meant anything now that all mine are used up. Felix had to have known this was going to happen. Why else would he rush me to make all three wishes right away? Without any time to really think of what I wanted, the wishes I made seemed to be haphazardly thrown together. Like a quick patch job. Get in, get it done, get out.

Except Felix didn't get out. Not really. His lamp is sitting on my desk, still and silent as if taunting me, knowing full well that

I can't make that genie come out.

It makes me so mad that I wasn't given the full story. I was duped and I feel like an idiot. I should've seen it coming. I suspected this outcome but the allure of having everything I wanted—what I *thought* I wanted—was too much to pass up.

Anger bubbles in me and I get up and snatch the lamp from the desk. I rub the side of it. If my life is stuck like this, I need that confirmation from Felix. He'll tell me that he knew this would happen. I'll make him.

I rub the lamp with such intensity I'm surprised I don't rub off the gold-plated rim at the top.

Nothing happens.

I press harder and rub faster until I can feel the heat of the friction between my fingers and the porcelain.

Still nothing.

I lift it and am about to hurl it at the wall, but stop when I smell sandalwood. The next moment, I see the familiar blue smoke start to seep out.

"Whoa! Easy there!" he says after he materializes next to me. "That's my house, I only get one!"

"You tricked me," I mutter in an attempt to keep my voice down.

"No, I didn't."

"You pushed me to make all three wishes as soon as possible so you could wreak havoc and get out of here before I could reverse them!"

"All I did was grant the wishes you asked for." He sits back on my bed and crosses his legs. "It's not my fault your life is a mess."

"Leo?" My mom calls from the next room. "Are you okay?"

"Fine!" I wait a minute and lower my voice further. "Your wishes have an expiration. My first wish? The money's out of my hands. My second? My dad's *still* an asshole. And my third wish? Turns out Violet never liked me. Just decided to call me out of the blue." Not to mention how upset Gen is...

"What I'm hearing is that your first wish is *still* going to help you out, you just have to wait. Have some patience. Your second wish was fulfilled because I *did* bring your parents back together. Sometimes things just aren't meant to be. You can't force fate. And you only asked for a date with that girl for your third wish. Not that she'd actually like you back."

I glare at him with my hands on my hips, searching for a retort. I don't have one. He's right. Technically, he fulfilled his end of the bargain. I should've been more careful with my wishes. I thought I was. I guess the lesson here is to never trust a genie. A statement I never thought I'd actually say.

"Get your feet off my bed," I demand. My anger is the only thing I have to cling to and I plan to go down fighting. No matter how petty it makes me.

He swings his legs over to the floor and gets up. "Happy?"

"No, I'm not happy. I want you to reverse the wishes. Take them all back. I don't care if it makes me poor again or if it leaves me wondering 'what if.' I just want them reversed."

Felix chuckles as I make my demands and shakes his head. "No can do, kiddo."

"Why not?" I wish he wouldn't call me 'kiddo.' Makes it seem like he can walk all over me.

"There's no take backs. You got your three wishes and now my services are done. I'm only standing here right now so you don't smash my house against the wall."

I hear the sound of the fridge open in the next room and I step closer to Felix and murmur, "Maybe I'll smash it anyway."

"Pass it off to someone else, sure. Lock me away for decades, fine. But breaking my lamp will give you *severely* bad luck for the rest of your life. Might even result in an early death." He shrugs. "Just thought I'd warn you. The last thing you'd want to do is piss off a genie."

"But this isn't the way it's supposed to go!" I sink into my bed and bury my head in my hands.

"Listen, kid, I'm sorry things didn't turn out the way you thought they would. Life generally sucks. Your mistake was wishing for things out of your control. Most people just wish to be thin forever or for a new car. Besides the money, you wished for other people to change. Seems to me like you just want a new life."

Not a new life. My old one. I was much happier before I ever met Felix. Before I made those wishes. Broke, sure, but at least the people who cared about me were happy.

I consider breaking his lamp out of spite. Right in front of him to see the look on his face turn from a conceited smile to shock. But the potential for a lifetime of bad luck scares me. Even if he is lying. I can't take that risk. Instead, I'll get rid of it. Hopefully it'll end up somewhere that'll leave Felix trapped inside for a long time.

"Get back in the lamp," I tell him. He gives me a suspicious look and I add, "I won't smash it. Promise."

"Then I guess this is goodbye. Again." With a bow, the air fills with the scent of sandalwood as his body dissipates into blue smoke and drifts back through the lamp's spout.

As soon as he's gone, I carry it downstairs and out to the trash cans around back. I turn to head back to the apartment, but my mother calls to me from the window.

"Tomorrow morning's trash day. Put the cans by the curb."

Grumbling, I drag our oversized trash can up to the street and nearly crash into my neighbor Bruce on my way back to the staircase.

"Oh, sorry," I mutter.

"No problem." He rubs the spot on his belly where I ran into him and then stuffs his bag in his own trash can. He calls to me as I walk away. "Hey, you're friends with Genevieve, right?"

"Gen? Yeah, we're friends." Not sure how true that is anymore, but best to keep conversations with Bruce to a minimum.

"What's going on with her? Her mother called me and said she skipped out of school early."

I feel a flash of heat and look down to the sidewalk. "Oh, I don't know. I thought she might be sick."

"Apparently she didn't *look* sick. I haven't seen her myself, though."

I shrug. "I don't know then."

"Maybe it's her girly time. Women can get pretty high-strung, you know what I mean?" He slaps my arm and chuckles.

I give him a tight smile. "Well, I have a lot of homework to do. I'll see you later."

I head back inside and attempt to start on my physics lab, but I can't concentrate. What Bruce said about Gen distracts me. Is she really that upset about me hanging out with Violet? Why didn't she tell me she liked me before? *Does* she like me or am I reading too much into it?

I guess I haven't been completely truthful with her, either. I never told her about Felix. Fear of looking stupid. Well, that ship has sailed for me. Maybe I should just tell her about finding the lamp. She was with me when I bought it. Of course, I doubt Felix would come out of his lamp for me *again*. Especially after he warned me about the eternal bad luck.

Would she believe me without any proof? That might be the test of our friendship. Then again, she might think that I'm making fun of her. I definitely don't want that. I don't really know what I want.

What I do know is I need to apologize to her. But first I need to make it clear that things between Violet and me are done.

Chapter Eight

GEN'S NOT IN school today. Last night she wouldn't return my texts or answer any of my calls. I should've just gone over there last night to apologize but I still have to figure out how exactly I'm going to do that. Words don't seem like they'd be enough, but maybe that's all I need.

The school day seems to drag on without her. Without anyone, really. For the first time I finally realize how lucky I was to have her with me. Why would I want to risk that with a stupid wish? For a stupid date with a stupid girl who didn't even like me.

That's all over now. Felix's lamp is probably on its way to the dump, likely to be put in a landfill and buried for God only knows how long.

Good riddance.

I don't need him. Never really did. Now's the time to start cleaning up the mess he left in his wake. I never should've trusted

"

that he'd make my life any better. I should've gone with my gut feeling: the wishes were too good to be true.

The warm weather means the sidewalk on the way home from school is full of kids running around, laughing, enjoying the nice May day. I'm not enjoying it nearly as much as they are. In fact, the other kids are kind of getting on my nerves simply because they're carefree while I'm miserable. It's only the funk I'm in, I know, but it only adds to everything else I'm going through. Luckily, I don't live far from the school so my walk is short.

As I approach the apartment, grateful to finally separate myself from the rowdy group I'd been following, I notice Bruce pull into his driveway in a slick red sports car. That's new.

He sees me staring when he stops and smiles widely. "She's a beaut, isn't she?"

"Yeah, very nice." Curious myself, I walk over to take a look. Leather seats, tinted windows, chrome rims. The whole nine yards. "When did you get this? Gen never mentioned anything about you getting a new car."

"She doesn't know yet. It was a, uh, gift."

I narrow my eyes. "A gift?" Must be nice to have rich friends.

"Yeah, just picked it up today. Do you want a ride?"

Shaking my head, I say, "Maybe some other time. I have a lot of homework to get to."

"Suit yourself. You're missing out."

I turn to head back to my place and notice the empty trash can sitting by the curb.

According to Gen, money was tight for her dad. He's missed a few of the checks to her mom. And she never mentioned anything about rich friends or relatives.

Why on earth would someone buy Bruce a car? Not to mention one like that.

Spinning on my heels, I turn back toward Bruce, who's eyeing me suspiciously. Cautiously. Warily.

"Where did you say you got this car?" I ask.

"A friend."

"What friend?"

He waves it off. "Oh, one of my friends from high school."

"Why did he buy you a car?"

"What's with the sudden interest in my friends?"

"Just answer the question," I push.

He crosses his arms and eyes me up, likely trying to make himself look more intimidating. I don't fall for it.

"Why don't you ask me what you really want to know?" he says.

"Did you steal something from our trash bin yesterday?"

"What makes you say that?"

"I think you know."

He gives me a nervous smile. "You're not dumb, kid. What did you ask for?"

"Doesn't matter. Give it back."

Bruce laughs. "Why would I give it back? I still have two more wishes. Felix is basically my slave until then."

"He's *not* a slave."

He chuckles. "Oh yeah? Isn't that why he calls me 'master'?"

"He calls everyone that. What are you even going to wish for?"

"None of your damn business. Now go run off and do your homework or go play or something."

"But—"

"But nothing, kid. Get!" He points to my apartment.

Fresh out of options, I turn and slowly make my way back home.

Chapter Nine

MOM IS WORKING so it's just me and a bowl of soup for dinner. I eat slowly as I let my mind wander. I can't imagine someone like Bruce with the unlimited magic of someone like Felix. The sports car is only the beginning. The second wish will likely test the limits of Felix's power and then the third wish will be through the roof. Like eternally profitable investments or something similar.

And the way he called Felix his 'slave' doesn't sit well with me. It just goes to show that Bruce has no intention of wishing for something that he'd share with people around him. People who need it.

I break some crackers into my soup and push them down with the bottom of my spoon as the worry strikes me that I was just as greedy when I made my wishes. But it's not the same.

I only wished for money to help my mom out, not so I could get rich. *She* decided to set it aside in a college fund for me. And

All I Ever Wanted

I asked for my parents to get back together to make *her* happy. Bruce isn't going to think of anyone but himself when he makes his wishes. Felix should go to someone who isn't so selfish.

Okay, so maybe a part of me also wants to see Felix go to someone who's nicer. All I know is that I need to get that lamp back.

The problem is, I have no idea where Bruce is keeping it and even if I did, I don't know what I'd do with that piece of information. If I took it, he'd know it was me. I could ask Gen for help. She might be able to sneak in and find it without drawing too much attention.

But would she even do it? Even if she did, wouldn't it raise suspicion? She doesn't usually come to his house.

I finish off my soup and put the clip back on the package of crackers. I look out the window as the last rays of the setting sun stretches over the rooftops and consider how stable my plan is— it's not. There are too many 'ifs' to make it work. Like Gen forgiving me, her believing me about Felix, her willing to help me, and her father not asking too many questions.

Of course, I'd still have to think about what I'd do once Bruce realized the lamp is gone. There'd be some sort of retaliation. How am I going to keep him at bay without Felix's magic at my disposal? I wish I had more wishes to use.

There's that word again. Wish. Haven't I learned enough already this week? Wishing for things I don't need got me into this predicament. More wishes won't get me out.

First thing's first, though: apologizing to Gen. I take my bowl to the sink and rinse it out before grabbing my keys and setting off toward her house. From the window at the top of the stairs, I see Bruce out on a lawn chair in his driveway watching his car with a beer in his hand.

To avoid any further suspicion, I take the long way around the block and head further down Main Street to Gen's mother's house.

It takes me an extra twenty minutes and when I arrive, it's completely dark outside, save for the streetlights.

"Leo, hi, come in," her mother says when she answers the door. "We just finished dinner. If I knew you were coming, I would've made extra."

She has her hair pulled back in a bun and she's still wearing her dress pants and shirt from work. Usually a few times a month I have dinner over here because Ms. Callaghan knows how weird my mom's shifts are. Plus, they live right down the street from my apartment. Used to be only two houses down.

"No, it's okay," I say with a smile. "I was actually hoping to talk to Gen. If she's home."

"Yeah, she's inside." She leads me back to the kitchen where Gen is elbow-deep in dirty dishes as she scrubs at a plate from her dinner.

"Hey," I start.

"Hey," she says into the sink.

"Can we talk? Outside?"

Sensing the tension, her mother pushes Gen aside and says, "Go ahead. I'll finish these. Thank you, dear."

Gen dries her hands and follows me out onto the front porch. We sit in the swing that's usually occupied by her mother.

"Leo, don't worry about what happened. I'm being—"

"No, I was wrong," I interject. "I'm sorry for going out with Violet. I didn't know you liked me. As your friend, I probably should've realized that."

She sighs. "Well, as your friend, I probably should've *told* you."

"Yeah, might've helped some." I smirk, which she returns.

"Why did you go out with her? It was so random. This has been such a weird week for you."

My heart beats faster as I consider how I want to tell her. It's almost as if there's a physical wall holding back this secret. We both know something's coming, but it's up to me to tell her. Push this thing over the wall so we both can see.

"Well…you need to keep an open mind about this. I'm not lying or joking or losing my mind. I promise."

"Well…" she jokes but stops when she sees my look. "Okay, I'll keep an open mind. What's up?"

"You remember that gravy boat I got for my mom last weekend?"

"Yeah, what about it?"

"Turns out it wasn't *really* a gravy boat. It was a, um…" Here goes nothing. "It was a genie lamp."

A burst of laughter escapes her. "What?"

"Open mind, remember?"

She puts up her hands, a grin still present. "Okay."

"I got three wishes, like you'd expect. I was skeptical at first, but he appeared out of thin air. This genie-dude with shiny pants and a turban."

Her smile grows. "A genie, sure. Wouldn't be complete without the turban."

"I'm being serious!" I knew convincing her would be a challenge. "The first wish was for money, which was how I got that college fund. The next was for my parents to get back together—big mistake. And the third was to go on a date with Violet."

Her smile fades. "Oh."

"That's why it seemed out of the blue, because it was. Violet claimed she'd been thinking about me—"

"Probably making fun of you. She always does. Everyone knew it. At least, the girls did."

"Oh."

"Yeah."

Well, there goes that angle. I scramble for a different approach to comfort Gen.

"Yesterday at school she was different from the night before," I say. "Cold, standoffish."

"Well, yeah, she's Violet Dolan. She plays those games. Wants guys chasing her. Probably the only reason she called you. You're so clueless sometimes."

No argument there. I had no idea that my own best friend had feelings for me. And now? All I can think about is that stupid genie.

"So where is this alleged genie friend of yours now that you're done with all three wishes?" I can tell she's still just humoring me.

"Gen, I'm not joking around here. This is serious. Your dad called Felix his 'slave.'"

"Felix?"

"That's his name."

"Of course it is. Sounds like a cat's name to me."

"Yeah, well. Anyway, he told me that I was his first master to treat him like a real person."

"Master? Leo, this is getting ridiculous." She gets up and moves to the door.

"Fine, I'll just have to break into your dad's house by myself." I'm down the porch steps before she calls my name.

"Leo, wait! What do you mean you're going to break into my dad's house?" She leans against the porch fence.

"I was mad that my wishes didn't turn out the way I thought they would so I wanted Felix to reverse them. He wouldn't, so I threw his lamp in the trash, but…"

She raises her eyebrows. "But what?"

"I think your dad stole it."

"Why do you think that?"

"He must've seen it in our trash can when I took them out last night. Then this afternoon he pulls up with a fancy new car."

She looks at me with wide eyes. "Is *that* how he got that stupid car?"

"I think so. Have you seen it?"

"No, but he's been sending me pictures. Said he wants to take me for a ride." She pulls out her phone and comes down the steps to show me. There has to be at least twenty pictures. The outside of the car at various angles, a couple of Bruce sitting behind the wheel, and some interior shots.

It takes a moment, but we both become very aware of how close we're standing. How my hand brushes against hers as I steady the phone to take a look. There's a weird burning feeling in my stomach and suddenly Felix is the furthest thing from my mind.

Gen steps back and clears her throat, which breaks me out of my trance.

"Right, well, your dad has it," I say. "And I don't think that's good. Not with what he called Felix or how he's going to use his wishes."

She sighs, reluctant to take this seriously. "If this lamp *does* exist and my dad *does* have it, he'll be a total prick about it. He's greedy. Something that'll get him lots of attention and money. He's been so desperate for money lately that he'll do anything—and I bet he won't even pay my mom what he owes her."

We're quiet as we watch a couple of kids from our school whiz down the street on their bikes. It's one of the first warm nights of the year.

"You don't believe me about Felix, do you?"

"I don't know, Leo…"

"He's, uh…goofy."

She smiles. "I'm sure you loved that."

"Not exactly. He's kind of annoying."

"Well, he's a boy, so…" She pushes me away playfully.

"Noted," I say with a grin. "Anyway, I asked your dad if he had the lamp and he basically confirmed that he did, but he wasn't willing to give it up."

"Would *you* give it up?"

"Actually, yeah."

She rolls her eyes with a smile. "Well, you're a freak."

I face her. "I need your help, Gen. I need you to get the lamp away from your dad so he doesn't wish for something stupid."

"Like what?"

"Like…getting your mom to get back together with him."

"She wouldn't," she says, turning away from me.

"Sure she would. Mine did."

"How's that working?"

I let out a breath of air. "Horribly. He already took off."

"Of course he did."

"But if I didn't interrupt their fight, he might've…" My voice trails off. I don't want to think about it. "Felix can make *anything* happen. When he's forced to obey someone like your dad, that could have lasting effects for everyone connected to him. We need to stop him. Will you help me?"

She looks up at me with a hint of a smile. "Yes, I'll help."

Chapter Ten

I T DIDN'T TAKE long to determine the plan. Gen didn't seem to think her dropping by unannounced would raise too much suspicion.

"I could say I want to check out his car," she says as we walk back toward her dad's house.

"Didn't you already ignore all of his texts? He's going to wonder why you just showed up."

"My dad doesn't take that much interest in me."

"He knows we're friends."

She scrunches her eyebrows together. The streetlights cast shadows on her face. "He does?"

"Yeah, he asked me about you the other day. He could tell that you were upset."

"Oh."

"Sorry again about that."

"It's fine."

We walk for a bit without either of us speaking, but as Bruce's house draws nearer, I'm forced to break the silence.

"You could say you forgot something inside. Maybe a sweater or something."

"I don't usually leave anything at his place."

"Or maybe he'll be so distracted with showing you the car that I can sneak inside."

She shakes her head. "What if he catches you?"

"What if you find the lamp but can't sneak it past him?"

"Touché. We can try it your way. He usually leaves the back door open. But…the only way to the back yard is from the front." She chews on the inside of her lip.

We're only a few houses down now, so we need to come up with something quick.

"No loose fence board or anything?"

"I don't know, Leo! I don't like coming here. We usually just sit and watch TV or something."

I consider our circumstances. Both mine and Gen's parents aren't together, but at least my father is gone. Gen, despite her ill feelings toward her dad, is still forced to see him. If I had to choose, I'd pick my situation over hers. After my second wish, though, I doubt my dad will ever come back. In that sense, maybe Felix actually helped me.

Yeah, like I'd ever admit that to him. Of course, we have to get his lamp from Bruce before I can say anything to him.

"Okay, here's what we're going to do." I stop her on the sidewalk. "You distract him long enough for me to get around to the backyard and get inside. Once I'm in, chat him up for a little bit—"

"How long's a little bit?"

"I don't know, let's say five, ten minutes to be safe?"

She lets out a deep breath. "I'll try."

I look in the direction of Bruce's house, only two houses over. It's now or never. I'm starting to get nervous.

"Thank you for helping me," I say.

"Of course, you're my best friend."

I look down at the ground because I can feel my face flush with heat. I notice her hands resting on her side and consider taking one in mine, but now's not the time. We have work to do before her dad decides to head in for the night.

"Should I look in any particular place inside?"

She sucks in her bottom lip as she considers this. "Hmm… maybe his bedroom closet. Back when he still lived with us, he used to stash my Christmas presents in there. But now that he's alone, I don't know."

I nod, trying not to worry about finding it in time. "Okay. I'll look there."

"Leo," she grabs my hand when I turn to continue down the sidewalk, "be careful."

I squeeze her hand back. "I will, don't worry. It's just your dad." I leave out the fact that he's got control of genie and two wishes left to use. What if he decides to use one of them against me?

Ignoring the thought, I wave for Gen to go first and I tuck behind a bush in the neighbor's yard until I hear them in the garage.

Bruce does most of the talking. Mostly about his car. Gen doesn't ask too many questions about where it came from. Rather, she asks about the features and the year and mileage. I wouldn't have thought to do that, so it's a good thing she came along.

Peeking around the corner, I see they're both turned toward the house. Gen's pointing to the top and I hear something about Christmas lights. I don't have a chance to see if Bruce's house is still adorned with holiday cheer before I race behind his car. Crouching along the side, I hope that they're still facing the other way so I can sneak—

"Come on, let me give you a ride," I hear him tell her.

"Uh, sure. Yeah," she says.

Scooting around the corner, I duck out of sight until I hear them drive off a few minutes later.

I check to make sure the coast is clear before I zip to the backyard. Once behind the garage, I lean forward on my knees, my butt resting against the wall of the garage, and try to steady my breathing.

The backdoor is locked, but the window beside it is open. Not a lot, but I think I might be able to squeeze. Luckily, he doesn't have a dog.

Using the trash cans beneath the window as a step, I manage to worm my way inside and crash to the floor. Not the most ideal, but at least I'm in. My nerves are on high-alert. I have no idea how long Bruce and Gen's joyride will last.

Although the room is dark, illuminated only by a single nightlight on the opposite wall, I can tell I'm in what's probably the living room. To the left is the kitchen and a single light above the sink is the only thing on. A bathroom divides the living room and the kitchen. Opposite the kitchen are doorways to two small bedrooms with a large freestanding bookshelf between them.

It doesn't take long to figure out which bedroom is Bruce's. The one that isn't used as storage. Gen doesn't even have a room if she *did* want to spend the night.

Stepping into the bedroom, Felix's lamp is the first thing I see sitting on the bedside table. I grab it just as I hear the car pull back into the driveway.

I drop to the floor and stash the lamp underneath, shifting some boxes to further conceal it. Back on my feet, I move to the closet and try to squeeze my way behind the sliding doors but the space is crammed with too much stuff.

"No, I'm not hungry," Gen says, her voice growing louder as they enter the house. "I just had dinner at Mom's."

With no other choice, I duck behind the bedroom door.

"I have to show you something, but promise you won't tell anyone." Bruce's voice grows louder still.

The bedroom light clicks on.

"Dad! No!"

Doing my best to stay completely still, I watch as Bruce takes two steps to the bedside table before he realizes the lamp is gone. He turns to leave the room and his eyes land on me. His nostrils flare with anger.

He lunges at me and grabs me by my shirt.

"Come here, you little creep! You looking for that genie, huh?" His face is inches from mine.

Gen tugs at his arm. "Dad, come on, leave him alone! He's leaving right now!"

He turns on her. "Did you know about this? Is that why you've been asking so much about the car? Why you wanted to go for a longer ride? To keep me outside?"

Tears well up in her eyes. "Dad, I'm so sorry!"

"Where is it?" He pushes Gen off of him and releases me.

He opens the closet door and dumps out a box on his bed. All that falls are various knickknacks and a few stray pens. Unsatisfied, he tosses the box in our direction and tears through the rest of his closet, throwing out clothes, shoes, even wiping off the top shelf completely.

"Tell me where the hell it is!" he bellows once the closet is empty.

"I don't know," I lie. "I couldn't find it."

"You moved it, didn't you?" Getting down on his knees in front of the closet, he swings his arm under his bed with his cheek pressed against the mattress.

I hold my breath as he searches, hoping his hand doesn't land on the lamp.

"Come on, just hand it over!" He gets to his knees with a grunt.

I shake my head again without a word.

He pushes past Gen and moves to the bedroom door. "Unbelievable."

She moves to follow him but he stops her just before she crosses the threshold.

"You two wanted to get in here so bad, you can stay in here." The door slams and we hear the distinct sound of the large bookshelf sliding in front of the door.

Gen pounds at the door. "Dad! Let us out!"

"Tell me where you stashed the lamp and you're free to go!"

Looking over at Gen, I can tell she's considering it, but I shake my head no.

"You're going to lock us up over a stupid lamp?" I ask.

"You had your chance!" Bruce shouts from the other side. "Now's my turn!"

Chapter Eleven

GEN AND I push at the bookshelf, trying to topple it over so we can escape but it doesn't budge. There's too much on it. Throughout our efforts, we can hear Bruce in the next room, rifling through more boxes. Looking for Felix's lamp.

Finally, Gen gives up and groans.

"This isn't going to work!"

"Should we call the police?" she asks.

"And what would we offer as the reason for breaking into *his* house?"

She shrugs. "I don't know, Leo, but we need to figure *something* out!"

"Could we call your mom?"

"And risk her thinking I'm a psycho? Yeah right."

"Won't your dad tell her about this?" I ask.

"She's not going to believe him. Besides, he wouldn't tell her because then he'd have to tell her about the lamp too."

"Well, we need to come up with something. We can't just sit here."

"What about the window?"

I grin. "Good idea."

We both clamber over to the window only to be nearly face-to-face with her father on the other side of the glass. I didn't even notice the noise in the next room stop.

"Hand over the lamp and I'll let you out," he says.

Gen shrieks and pulls the curtains closed. "Where *is* the lamp?" she whispers to me.

I reach under the bed and dig through the mess Bruce made until I get ahold of it. "Here."

She cocks an eyebrow. "So this is it, huh?"

"Yeah."

"Still looks like it's just a gravy boat."

"Well, it's not. It's a genie lamp."

"Then tell him to get out here and help us." She grabs it from me and shakes it.

"Hey! Careful!" I warn.

Her hand slips over the porcelain and the room fills with the scent of sandalwood as the familiar blue smoke begins to erupt from the spout. Felix's body takes form from the smoke and moves to the floor beside us.

Gen takes a step back and grabs my arm with a vice-like grip.

"Why, hello there," the genie says to Gen with a bow. "I'm Felix. Your wish is my command."

"My—what?" Her mouth hangs open as she stares. "Is this— you were just—how—what?"

I laugh. "This is Felix. The genie."

He nods to me.

"Believe me *now*?" I gloat.

She continues to stare with her mouth wide open.

Felix leans over to me with his eyes on Gen and mutters, "She's a strange one, isn't she?"

I roll my eyes. "She's just shocked."

He claps his hands and stands up straighter. "Well, judging from your predicament, I'd say you need me now more than ever."

"So you can help me?" I smile widely.

"Eh, 'no." He points to Gen. "I can help *her*. Even though she's short a few marbles, I'd say she's world's ahead of my last master. He was—"

"Scary?" I offer.

Felix nods. "And mean."

"Yeah, well, that's mostly my fault," I admit. "I tried to throw your lamp out and Bruce must've taken it. Sorry about that."

He shrugs. "Better than breaking it. Then I would've had to kill you." His face is serious for a moment while I stare at him with worry. Finally, he doubles over and laughs. "You should've seen your faces! So gullible!"

"Leo, what's going on?" Gen finally asks.

She snaps me back to reality and I turn to Felix. "Right, well, we tried to get your lamp away from Bruce, but we sort of got ourselves stuck."

He looks at the blocked door and curtained windows. "I see that. By Mr. Mean-Man?"

I nod. "Can you get us out?"

He scrunches his nose. "No can do, mister. Like I said, you've used all your wishes."

"But I have three wishes, right?" Gen asks cautiously.

Felix looks around the room and then back to her. "Who did you think I was talking to when I said, 'Your wish is my command'?" He bows again.

She smiles despite herself. "Well, there we go."

"Gen." I reach for her hand to get her full attention.

"Remember what I told you about my wishes?"

"Yeah, but I could wish—"

"Watch the *W* word!"

"I could *get* us out of here," she continues with an eye roll, "and then still have two left for me."

"Except…what's stopping your dad from finding the lamp again and getting his other two wishes?"

She sighs. "Fine, I'll use one to get rid of the lamp too. That still leaves one for me."

"Genie blocking," Felix says to Gen with a smirk. "Impressive."

"Gen, please be careful with your wishes."

"I'll be fine, Leo."

"So are you ready then?" Felix asks her.

She stands and says, "For my first wish, I wish that our path out of this house was no longer blocked."

Felix snaps his fingers and we hear loud banging from outside the door as the bookshelf begins to slide out of the way on its own.

"What the hell?" Bruce shouts from the other side of the door.

As the bookshelf moves, it reveals a disheveled house and Bruce standing among the wreckage. He's been busy looking for the lamp.

"Go!" I tell Gen. "Hold onto the lamp!"

Bruce runs at us as we move to the door, but he bounces back onto the floor as if we're surrounded by an invisible rubber forcefield.

"Genie, stop them!" he commands.

"Well, you see, sir, you didn't *actually* make a wish so I'm afraid I…" Felix babbles to Bruce while we escape.

Booking it across the yard, we barely make it to the end of the driveway before Bruce is shouting at us from the front door.

"Genevieve, stop!"

Gen slows, but I tug on her arm. "Come on!"

We make it to the staircase leading up to my apartment before he catches us. Halfway up, I feel a hand grasp my ankle and pull me down on his way up.

"Out of my way," he grumbles to me as he passes by. "Genevieve!"

Trying to ignore my swelling tongue from biting it, I struggle to keep myself up on the staircase. Scrambling to my feet, I follow Bruce up to my apartment. He's at my bedroom door, pleading with his daughter to let her in.

"Genevieve, come on. Let me use those last two wishes. Open up and give me the lamp. I'll wish for something we both can enjoy. You'd like a car, wouldn't you?"

"Gen, don't listen to him!" I call to her. "Get rid of it! The wishes won't turn out the way you want them to."

Ignoring Felix, Bruce turns to me with fire in his eyes.

"*Don't* get rid of it, sweetie," he says to her with his eyes locked on me. He lowers his voice and steps closer to me. "You think you can get your three wishes and not let anyone else get theirs? What makes you so special?"

I back into the living room. "I didn't know what I was doing, either. I never should've made those wishes."

"Then you should've reversed them," he says, stepping closer. "I *tried*!"

He waves his fingers toward him. "Okay, sure. Then give me some of that money you got."

My back hits the wall. "What? No."

"You didn't earn it yourself." He puts his one arm on the wall just above my shoulder, pinning me in place. "What does a kid like you need with all of that money?"

"It's for college."

Bruce scoffs. "Please, don't even give me that bull."

"It wasn't even supposed to go to me! I just wanted to give my mom a break," I tell him. "You just want to help yourself."

Bruce jabs his finger into my chest and looks like he's about to retort, but Gen's voice stops him.

"It's over," she says in a small voice. She's standing by the dining room table with the lamp in her hand and Felix by her side.

He turns to look at her. "What do you mean it's over? Give me the lamp and we'll forget this happened."

"Nothing good will come from any one person having this kind of power." She turns to Felix. "I wished your lamp to be sealed away forever, only to found by someone who's truly selfless." She adds, "Sorry, Felix."

"No!" Bruce shouts. "Genie, I wish that you'd stay!"

Felix nods at her. "No hard feelings." He looks at me with sad eyes. "It's been fun kid." With a snap of his fingers, he and the lamp disappear in a puff of blue smoke.

Silence and sandalwood fills the room after he leaves as both Bruce and I stare dumbfounded at Gen, both for different reasons.

"You just *wasted* an opportunity!" Bruce moves toward her and I'm afraid he's going to hit her with how angry he is, but he doesn't.

"Just go enjoy your car," she says.

His chest heaves as he stares at her. He casts one last look at me and then walks out and stomps down the stairs.

Approaching her, I hesitate for a moment before pulling her into an embrace.

"What made you give up your last two wishes?" I ask.

"Greed. I felt a shift in me as soon as I released Felix and thought I might have a couple wishes to myself. I didn't like it. Nothing worth having comes easy."

Chapter Twelve

I NEVER FOUND a replacement gift for Mother's Day. Instead I decided to get up early to make her breakfast. I figure after everything we've been through this past week, we could both use a day to relax and unwind. She actually has the day off, too.

"Oh, honey, this look delicious," she says when she emerges from her bedroom. She gives me a hug and kisses my cheek. "Thank you for this."

"Of course. Happy Mother's Day." I set a plate with a big Belgian waffle in front of her. "Syrup or jelly?"

"Syrup." She sits down and pulls the plate toward her.

I set two glasses of orange juice on the table and join her.

We eat in silence for a little bit. Usually we talk about school or work, but none of that compares to the debacle I've been through this week with Felix. And Mom's probably still beating herself up over Dad.

"I like this," I say.

"Mmm," she mumbles with a mouthful. "It's good."

"No, this." I wave between us. "Just you and me. That's all we need."

Her face droops. "I'm sorry for bringing your father back into the picture."

I shake my head. "No, it's okay. I understand. You needed to see if he's changed. He hasn't. No harm done, not really. Everyone makes mistakes. We just have to learn to move on."

She smiles. "When did you get so grown up?"

I roll my eyes. "Let's not make this a Hallmark moment."

Stabbing her waffle, she sits up straights and says with a grin, "Right, sorry."

Another quiet moment fills the room. Finally, I ask, "You're happy, right?"

"Why do you ask?"

"Well, the first time Dad left, you were really upset and I just thought—"

"This time is different. We already know what it's like without him. Before I was nervous about how I'd handle everything. Now I know I can."

"So you're happy?"

She smiles and squeezes my hand. "Very."

"I LOVE YOUR front porch," Mom says as she and Gen's mom sway on the swing.

The sun is setting, but it's still warm. Since Gen and her mom were going to be alone for Mother's Day, I suggested the four of us get together. Plus, I wanted to see Gen.

"Oh, so do I," Ms. Callaghan replies. "I wish I could sit out here all year long."

"You pretty much do," Gen adds. "She'll sit out here like an

Eskimo if she has to." She mimes her mom sitting bundled up.

Everyone laughs. After a minute, Gen says, "I'm going to get more iced tea. Leo, can you help?"

It's a thinly-veiled excuse for us to be alone, but I jump at it and follow her to the kitchen.

We bump into each other several times as we move behind the kitchen island, the awkwardness between us evident. Still, she pretends nothing's wrong and refills the glasses. I sip mine and we look at each other.

"So," I start. Yup, definitely need to learn how to initiate an awkward conversation better.

"So…" She giggles and nurses her own glass.

"You got pretty jealous of Violet, huh?"

Her face drops. "Yes."

Oooh, just ruined the playfulness. Recover, Leo, recover.

"I like that you did."

She raises her eyebrows.

"Not—that's not—let me start again."

She giggles. That's a good sign.

"You're my best friend. I've always been able to tell you everything…until I realized that you had other feelings for me. That's when I started to pay attention to the way I looked around you. The way I acted, what I said. It's weird. I don't know what you're doing to me."

She cuts me off with a kiss. I can taste the sugar from the iced tea on her lips. When we part, I want to do it again, but decide we better not.

"Our moms are probably getting thirsty," she says.

I grin, knowing my face is probably so red. But I don't care. I follow her back out to the porch with that same goofy grin on my face.

"Well, that took you long enough," Gen's mother teases as we hand her and my mom their glasses.

"Sorry, we got distracted," Gen says.

As I settle in the chair beside her and reach for her hand, I realize that I didn't need Felix or any of his wishes to give me anything. I've always had all I ever wanted.

BEHIND THE BOOK:
All I Ever Wanted

All I Ever Wanted is the first standalone book I've released since my short story *Limelight* in 2016. Actually, this book and *Limelight* were published exactly two years apart (*Limelight* on May 7, 2016, *All I Ever Wanted* on May 7, 2018).

This book had a number of things against it from a business standpoint: it's a standalone, it's a novella, it's in the young adult genre, and it's unrelated to the series I just finished publishing or the series I'm about to publish.

Let me elaborate:

- **It's a standalone** - Being a standalone is a bad thing when it comes to sales because if readers like this book, there's nothing more for them to read in this series. From a business standpoint that means that if I spend X amount of advertising money to get people to buy this book, my profit is limited to just the sale of this book, whereas with a series, readers are more likely to continue to the next book.

- **It's a novella** - Readers typically want longer books. The fact that this isn't a novel-length book can turn some readers off.

- **It's in the young adult genre** - Young Adult is kinda-sorta where I started. I definitely marketed the Under the Moon books as YA, but they're not all *truly* YA. Actually, any YA book that I wrote prior to this (looking at you, *Snow After Christmas…*) was just a happy accident. The reason that this book being YA is a bad thing is because the YA market is super saturated now. Between *The Hunger Games*, *Divergent*, *The Maze Runner*, *The Fault in Our Stars*, and *Fangirl*, among so many others, readers of this genre have a lot to choose from and it's harder for a small indie like myself to really stand out in YA.

- **It's unrelated to the series I just finished publishing or the series I'm about to publish** - This one is pretty obvious, but let me dive in a bit. Prior to publishing this book, I put out the final book in my Fuse series, my first series in the superhero fiction genre. That means that I started to build up a fanbase of superhero readers. I don't have any immediate plans to publish future YA books (although never say never), so the fact that this book kind of comes in from the outfield doesn't bode well for its success. Likewise, I'm about to publish a string of romance novellas. Although All I Ever Wanted has a romance element to it (as do a lot of stories), it is not, at its core, a romance book.

All I Ever Wanted

Now, even with all of these things against it, I still chose to write it. Why? *Because I can.* What's the point of being an indie author if you can't throw out a random title once in a while? I came up with this idea a long time ago, outlined it, and just did it.

Okay, so here's some of the true "Behind the Book" details. I came up with the title for this book first. It was back in 2009 and a song called "All I Ever Wanted" came up on my iPod and I started thinking about how *All I Ever Wanted* would be such a good book title. Then I started piecing together the scenario in my head of a boy finding a genie and realizing that having everything he's ever wanted wasn't all it was cracked up to be.

Since I was still working on *The Blood Moon* and about to go to college, I wrote the notes down and shelved the idea until the summer of 2017 when I had some extra time on my hands in between books. I figured I'd write it in my spare time and wouldn't worry about length. However long it took to tell the story would be how long the book is.

So I wrote the first draft that summer, worked on the second draft in between edits of *Omertà* and writing *Oblivion* and finished it up at the beginning of 2018 after finishing another draft of *A Christmas Spark.*

Overall, I'm pretty satisfied with the way *All I Ever Wanted* turned out, especially since it kind of stands out on its own. I hope you enjoyed it! Please leave a review online and follow me on social media. I'm on Facebook, Twitter, and Instagram. (In all reality Instagram is the one I update the most. Facebook is mostly for new releases and progress updates and some signings. And Twitter? I don't even know why I have it…)

Even though this book doesn't *directly* lead into another book, it's similar to a few others I have. If you're digging the more fantasy stuff, pick up *The Full Moon,* the first in the Under the Moon series. If you're looking for something more YA with

a romance element and don't mind the holiday theme, pick up my short story *Snow After Christmas*. Or, if you want something completely different, you could pick up the first book in my Fuse series, *Origin*.

Thanks again for reading!

DavidNethBooks.com/Newsletter

Kathy and her sister, Samantha, have always been a team. Throughout their time as witches, they've taken out more than their share of bad guys. But after Kathy meets Will, who she learns is a demonic Dark Knight, her loyalties begin to change.

Meanwhile, Samantha doesn't trust Will or his intentions. Still, Kathy can't help but feel tempted by the dark side as she falls deeper in love with Will. Crossing over would give Kathy the freedom to do whatever she wanted with her magic. No rules. No limitations. It would also mean breaking the bond she has always shared with her sister, who has made it clear that she wants nothing to do with the dark side.

When Will proposes they take over the underworld, Kathy loves the idea of having power. But it also leaves her with a choice that will change her life: abandon her family and the life she has always known, or give up the love of her life forever.

Available in ebook, paperback, and audio!
DavidNethBooks.com/TheFullMoon

A chance moment. A snow storm. And the gift of a new beginning.

Tristan is ready to party and ring in the New Year by kissing his soon-to-be girlfriend, Julie. The only bad note in his rocking night is the growing snow storm. Outside his apartment, he's almost hit by Grace, the most beautiful woman with haunting green eyes. She's on her own mission to get home to her grandfather.

In a selfless act reminiscent of the age of knights and chivalry, Tristan vows to get her home...never realizing they are both on a date with destiny and their lives will be forever changed by the SNOW AFTER CHRISTMAS...

Available in ebook, paperback, and audio!
DavidNethBooks.com/SnowAfterChristmas

Ethan Pierce is just another IT tech support rep at Wyatt Industries until he's zapped and infused with enough electricity that should kill him. But electrocution has just given Ethan terrifying abilities that no man has ever had.

As he grapples with his strange new powers, he and his girlfriend Emma witness a drive-by shooting in the city of Olympia. They soon learn it was related to the Martelli crime family that run the city and don't like to leave loose ends.

Fearful of the threat of the family, Ethan and Emma try to lay low, but it's no use. When Emma is attacked, Ethan uses his newfound lightning abilities to become Fuse, Olympia's "man in black."

Fueled by vengeance and empowered by his new abilities, Ethan vows to find the man who attacked Emma and get justice. But will his powers be enough to save her?

Available in ebook, paperback, and audio!
DavidNethBooks.com/Origin

More by the Author

About the Author

David Neth is the author of the Fuse series, the Small Town Christmas series, the Under the Moon series, and other stories. He lives in Batavia, NY, where he dreams of a successful publishing career and opening his own bookstore.

Follow the author at

www.DavidNethBooks.com
www.facebook.com/DavidNethBooks
www.twitter.com/DavidNethBooks
www.instagram.com/dneth13

www.ingramcontent.com/pod-product-compliance
Lightning Source LLC
Chambersburg PA
CBHW051712180726
48283CB00004B/1312